MW00955586

Baby Doe

The mission of Wolgemuth & Hyatt, Publishers, Inc. is to publish and distribute books that lead individuals toward:

- A personal faith in the one true God: Father, Son, and Holy Spirit;

- A lifestyle of practical discipleship; and

- A worldview that is consistent with the historic, Christian faith.

Moreover, the Company endeavors to accomplish this mission at a reasonable profit and in a manner which glorifies God and serves His Kingdom.

Text © 1989 by Mary Pride. All rights reserved.
Illustrations © 1989 by Wolgemuth & Hyatt, Publishers, Inc.
Published May 1990. First Edition
Printed in the United States of America
96 95 94 93 92 91 90   8 7 6 5 4 3 2 1

No part of this publication may be reproduced, stored in a retrieval system, or transmitted in any form by any means, electronic, mechanical, photocopy, recording, or otherwise, without the prior written permission of the publisher, except for brief quotations in critical reviews or articles.

Illustrations by Vic Lockman.

Wolgemuth & Hyatt, Publishers, Inc.
1749 Mallory Lane, Suite 110, Brentwood, Tennessee 37027.

Library of Congress Catalog Number: 90-12292

CC

C
PRI

Baby Doe

by Mary Pride

C 1989

FIRST CHRISTIAN CHURCH
Library
GLEN ELLYN, ILLINOIS

5917

Wolgemuth & Hyatt, Publishers, Inc.
Brentwood, Tennessee

Listen, my children, and you shall hear
The tale of an innocent baby deer.

She was born one day in the bloom of spring—
Such a frail and helpless little thing!
Most fawns can stand on the day they're born.
But Baby Doe just lay there—forlorn.

Her tiny legs
    And her little feet
       Wouldn't work;
All this baby could do was bleat.

Her mother looked down in her baby's eyes
With an awful fear and a wild surmise.
"Please stand up, PLEASE stand up, my baby!" she said.

And she gave Baby Doe a push with her head.
But it did no good;
Baby Doe sank down
In a helpless heap,
On the hopeless ground.

Her father came strutting so proud and strong
To see what was taking his wife so long.
But when he saw his newborn fawn
Lying there on the grassy lawn,
He knew right away that something was
wrong.

"Quick, call the doctor!" the mother cried,
    As her baby nuzzled at her side.
The doctor came right away on the run.
    "Doctor, please tell us, what can be done?"
He turned around, and his face was sour
As he spoke these words in that fateful hour.

"This doe can't walk,
And she'll never get better.
My advice is to face it
And just forget her.
    I never am wrong.
    I always am right.
Get rid of her now!
        Don't wait till tonight.

"If a deer can't walk,
If a deer can't run,
    A hunter will get her with his gun.
Since she's sure to die,
There's no reason why
    YOU should have to suffer and work and cry.
Leave her alone!
It's the thing to do!
    With luck, she'll be gone in a day or two."

FIRST CHRISTIAN CHURCH
Library
GLEN ELLYN, ILLINOIS

Baby Doe nuzzled for her mother's side—
But her mother had stepped away in pride.
"I've MY life to live! I won't be tied down
To a worthless,
Bleating,
Weakling fawn!"

Baby Doe looked for her father's face,
    But he'd already left that deathly place
And was roaming the forest,
      Wild and free,
        Avoiding responsibility.
"It's not MY fault!" her father thought.
    "If the experts say 'die,' why should I say 'not'?
Besides, I have better things to do
    Than to care for a deer that belongs in a zoo!"

Baby Doe looked around once more.
She was all alone on the forest floor.
No one to hear her bleating cry.
  Was this the end?
  Was she doomed to die?

Well, many small deer have ended that way,
For love grows cold when no one will pray—
But Baby Doe was in luck that day!

For along came Nick with his big boots on!
He was swinging an ax and singing a song.
As he tramped through the forest, he scared all the
        game,
For Nick's left leg was a wee mite lame.
He almost tripped on the tiny fawn.
        And when he had put his glasses back on,
He stared in surprise at the little deer
        Who had not fled when she heard him near.

"Now, here's something new!" old Nick exclaimed.
"I do believe this poor fawn is lame.
We have something in common, Miss, I believe.
So, if you'll allow me—by your leave . . ."

He scooped her up with his big strong arm
And took her home to his cozy farm.
He milked the goat
And gave her a drink
And made her a bed by the kitchen sink.

Now the days flew by for the doe and Nick,
And the autumn leaves were falling thick.
Nick said, "Little Miss, you are looking pretty
It's time for us both to visit the city!

I have work to do,
And you can come too!
Lots of places to go
      And people to meet!
            Lots of sights to see!
                  Lots of food to eat!
Are you ready to go? You'll love it, I think.
            We'll take everything but the kitchen sink!"

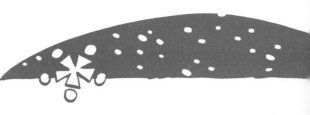

Snow was falling as Nick pulled in
To the parking lot where the shows begin.
Nick grabbed a blanket and hurried back
To carry his doe inside—on his back.
"The reindeer get lonely that work in this show.
You stick with them, Honey, while I work below."

Baby Doe had grown, but she still couldn't stand.
She put out her tongue and licked Nick's hand.
Then she settled down and looked around
At the wonderful place where she now was found.

The popcorn was popping!
The barkers were shouting!
    The children were having
    A wonderful outing!
The dancers were dancing,
The clowns were all playing,
    The reindeer prancing,
    The hound dogs baying!

The swingers were swinging from swing to swing
High above the dusty ring.
    And then it happened—a terrible thing!

The littlest swinger,
Whose name was Paul
Tried to catch a purple ball
Lost his grip
And began to fall!

The crowd hushed in horror
As he hurtled down!
Was it certain death
On the cold, hard ground?

Then something happened!
Something new!
Baby Doe rose up,
And away she flew!

She caught the boy
With a graceful swoop
Then did a beautiful
 Loop-the-loop.

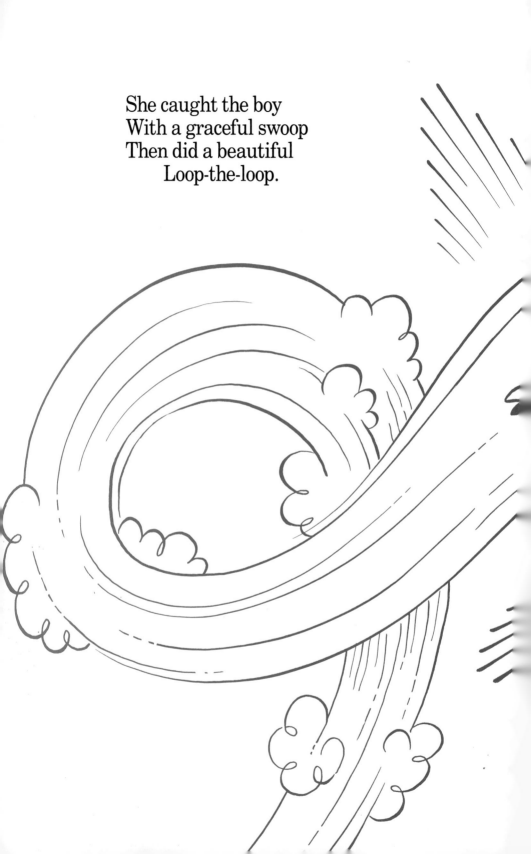

Paul was shouting and grinning.
The crowd went wild.
They cheered for the deer!
They cheered for the child!

Nick was so proud
Of his little deer!
You just should have heard him
Cheer, *cheer*, CHEER!

Baby Doe got a contract to star in the show,

And Nick got a contract to care for the doe.

Paul got to have the time of his life,

Nobody knows the reason why—
Baby Doe couldn't walk,
But she sure could fly!